AUSTRALIAN GEOGRAPHIC – WHERE GREAT GIFTS COME ALIVE

FOR MY BESTEST
GRANDAUGHTER

NOVEMBER 2017

Love ×××

Jumpy

in

Australia

AUSTRALIAN GEOGRAPHIC
STACKS OF GREAT GIFTS FOR EVERYONE

AUSTRALIAN GEOGRAPHIC
GREAT GIFTS FOR EVERYONE

MEET BLINKY BILL

Adapted from
Dorothy Wall's original story
by
Carol Odell

Illustrations based
on the original
Dorothy Wall characters
by
Louis Silvestro

CORNSTALK
PUBLISHING

The bush was alive with excitement. Mrs Koala had a brand new baby, and the news spread like wildfire. The kookaburras in the highest gum-trees heard it and laughed and chuckled; the rabbits came scuttling; Mrs Kangaroo fairly leapt in the air with joy; and even Mrs Snake, who was having a nap, awoke, gave a wriggle, and blinked her wicked little eyes.

In the fork of a gum-tree, far above the ground, Mrs Koala nursed her baby, peeping every now and then at the tiny creature in her pouch. He was only about an inch long and covered with soft baby fur. His mother and father always had a surprised look on their faces, but they looked more surprised than ever now as they gazed at their baby.

Every day he grew bigger and stronger, until he was six months old. Then his mother thought it quite time he learnt to ride on her back, as the pouch was getting too small to hold such a big baby.

Strange as it may seem, Mrs Koala had not thought of a name for him. "Shall we call him 'Walter' or 'Bluegum'?" she enquired.

"No," grunted Mr Koala. "Let's call him 'Blinky Bill'."

So Blinky Bill he became from that moment.

The Koala family lived so happily; never thinking of harm, or that anything could happen to disturb their little home. They had no idea such things as guns were in the world or that human beings had hearts so cruel.

Poor Mr Koala was curled up asleep when the terrible thing happened. Bang! And the man with the gun walked away, whistling as he went.

Mrs Koala waited a long time—then
she climbed slowly down the tree with
Blinky following close behind; great was their
surprise to find Angelina Wallaby waiting for them.

"Where are you going?" she asked.

"Far into the bush with Blinky, away from the man with his
gun," Mrs Koala replied.

"Come with us," grunted Blinky.

"Both of you hop on my back and we'll be there in no time," said Angelina. Away they went. It was great fun. Flop, flop, flop, through the grass, ducking their heads to miss the branches and twigs of low-growing trees, and then racing along through open country.

At last, breathless and tired, they stopped at the foot of a tall, straight gum-tree.

"How beautiful," murmured Mrs Koala. Slowly she crawled up the trunk with Blinky Bill on her back. A new tree was no joke. Everything seemed very quiet, but her eyes glistened as she looked at the young gum-tips.

Blinky was the first to discover other tenants in the tree.

"Look, mother," he whispered. "There's a little koala, just like me."

Sure enough, peeping at them from between leaves above their heads were two funny eyes and a small black nose.

"Hulloa," called Blinky.

"Hullo," replied the other, whose name was Snubby.

"Now you two young eucalyptus pots, run off and have a game," said Snubby's mother, Mrs Grunty. "I want to talk to Mrs Koala."

Blinky and Snubby needed no second bidding and were up in the branches in no time, dodging in and out of the leaves, and pelting everything visible with gum-nuts.

"Chew leaves quickly!" advised Snubby, as Blinky Bill hit Mrs Grunty on the nose by mistake.

The two naughty cubs looked the picture of innocence as they sat quietly perched on a limb chewing like two little cherubs.

"Must have been a stray nut falling," said Mrs Grunty. "They do sometimes."

The days and nights came and went, and Blinky grew into a strong koala. "Stuck in a tree all the time!" he grunted one day. "I'm for adventure. I've heard Mrs Grunty speak of motor cars and stores and all sorts of exciting things. Well I want to see for myself."

At the foot of the tree some of the braveness left him. The world seemed so large.

A cricket popped up, just at his feet. Blinky stood still with fright, his heart going pit-a-pat at a great rate.

"Great hoppers!" said the cricket. "A very bold lad, that's what I think you are."

"A fellow can't stay home all the time," replied Blinky.

"Well, take care you don't come to harm!" And the cricket hopped on its way.

Blinky set off, sometimes stopping to nibble at a plant that looked
extra sweet. It was a great adventure to taste something new
and smell the bush flowers.

After travelling many miles he began to feel tired, so he looked
around for a gum-tree where a little koala could have a nap in safety.
Finding just the kind he wanted, up he climbed, and there, in a cosy
fork between two branches, he cuddled up and went
to sleep—his head snuggled down on his
tummy, and his two front paws
folded over his ears.

Later he walked on and on until he felt his journey must be nearing its end. He could hear strange noises and smell the dust. He climbed up to a high branch to see what was in view. There just ahead of him was the road, and that surely must be the store. Here was adventure indeed! Waiting until all was quiet, he walked across the roadway and right on to the verandah. Over the door were large letters that looked like this: MISS PIMM. REFRESHMENTS.

Inside were rows and rows of strange things in tins and jars. And good gracious! there were some gum-tips in a bottle on the counter. Blinky Bill ate and ate those gum-tips. He scooped up a pawful of peppermints out of a jar, and cautiously tasted one of those, too. Finding it hot and very like some plants he had tasted in the bush, he ate more.

"Oh,
you robber!"
shrieked Miss Pimm, as she
caught sight of him. Blinky made a dart
round the counter and into a large tin of biscuits.
"You young scallywag! All my gum-tips gone as well!"
And she banged down the lid of the biscuit-tin with
an awful crash.

I must get out of here, thought Blinky, and waste no time about it.
Listening with his ear to the side of the tin, he heard Miss Pimm's
footsteps going towards the kitchen. He climbed out of the tin—and
dived into a sack of potatoes just as she came back through the door-
way. But she saw him!

Blinky was terrified. How he wished a gum-tree would spring up through the floor. He popped in and out of corners, over tins, under bags, with Miss Pimm after him. It was a terrible scuttle and in the middle of all the din Miss Pimm tripped over a broom and down she fell. Suddenly, all in a twinkling, Blinky saw a big bin standing open—he climbed up and dropped inside. It was full of oatmeal.

He wriggled and wriggled down as far as he could until he was quite hidden. All that could be seen was a little black nose breathing quickly. He kept his eyes closed very tightly and felt uncomfortable all over: but he was safe at last. Miss Pimm couldn't find him anywhere and, grumbling to herself, switched out the lights and locked the door. But, thank goodness, she forgot to lock the window.

Blinky could see the moon shining through the panes and he very, very quietly crawled out of the bin. A shower of oatmeal flew over the floor as he landed on his feet and shook his coat and ears.

Right on to the window-ledge he climbed, trod on all the apples that Miss Pimm had so carefully polished, sat down for a few moments on a box of chocolates, then, noticing more peppermints in the window, he pushed a pawful into his mouth and munched away in great content.

''Click!'' The store light went on.

''Bang! Crash!'' Blinky tumbled through the window.

''Pity he got away,'' he heard the policeman say to Miss Pimm, as he ran away down the road to safety.

Blinky thought it wise to go home before any more adventures came his way. Snubby's eyes nearly fell out of his head as he listened to Blinky's story later, as they sat in a fork of the tree whispering and giggling together.

With a twinkle in his eye, Blinky wondered what his next adventure in the wide world would bring.

CORNSTALK
An imprint of HarperCollins*Publishers*, Australia

First published in Australia by Angus & Robertson Publishers in 1970
New edition 1984
Reprinted in 1985, 1986, 1987, 1988, 1990
This Cornstalk edition published in Australia in 1991
Reprinted in 1996
by HarperCollins*Publishers* Pty Limited
ACN 009 913 517
A member of the HarperCollins*Publishers* (Australia) Pty Limited Group

HarperCollins*Publishers*
25 Ryde Road, Pymble, Sydney, NSW 2073, Australia
31 View Road, Glenfield, Auckland 10, New Zealand

National Library of Australia Cataloguing-in-Publication data:

Odell, Carol.
Meet Blinky Bill.
New ed.
Previous ed.: Sydney: Angus & Robertson, 1970.
Based on The complete adventures of Blinky Bill by Dorothy Wall.
For children
ISBN 0 207 14542 3.
I. Silvestro, Louis. II Wall, Dorothy.
The complete adventures of Blinky Bill. III. Title.
A82'.3

Printed in Singapore

12 11 10 9 8   96 97 98 99